Magic Animal Friends

To Tali, Sophie, and Amelia
The three brilliant beauties

Special thanks to Valerie Wilding

ORCHARD BOOKS
338 Euston Road, London NW1 3BH
Orchard Books Australia
Level 17/207 Kent Street, Sydney, NSW 2000
A Paperback Original

First published in 2014 by Orchard Books

A CIP catalogue record for this book is available
from the British Library.

ISBN 978 1 40834 845 1

5

Printed and bound in Great Britain by Clays Ltd, Elcograf S.p.A.

MIX
Paper from
responsible sources
FSC® C104740

Orchard Books is a division of Hachette Children's Books,
an Hachette UK company.

www.hachette.co.uk

Bella Tabbypaw in Trouble

Daisy Meadows

ORCHARD

Shining House
Sunshine Meadow
Blossom Briar
Toadstool Cafe
Goldie's Grotto
Toadstool Glade
Mrs Taptree's Library
Library
Friendship Tree
Maze
Silver Spring
Buttercup Grove
Lighthouse

Map of Friendship Forest

Can you keep a secret? I thought you could!
Then I'll tell you about an enchanted wood.
It lies through the door in the old oak tree,
Let's go there now - just follow me!
We'll find adventure that never ends,
And meet the Magic Animal Friends!

Love

Goldie the Cat

Contents

CHAPTER ONE

Kittens!

Lily Hart couldn't tear herself away from the box of kittens her dad had just brought into the examining room. Nor could her best friend, Jess Forester!

Lily's parents ran the Helping Paw Wildlife Hospital in Brightley, the village where the two girls lived. Jess and her dad lived in the house opposite the hospital. They'd found the kittens that morning in their shed and brought them straight to Helping Paw.

"I'll just check them over," said Mr Hart.

He picked up each of the four tabby kittens in turn, checking their eyes and teeth. When he put the smallest one back in the box, she rolled over on her back and mewed, showing the tip of a tiny pink tongue. Lily tickled her tummy.

"We were amazed to find them," Mr Forester said. "Jess heard barking and saw a dog chasing a cat away from the shed. It must have been the kittens' mother. When she didn't come back, we looked inside and found the kittens."

"We've put leaflets through everyone's letterboxes to find out who the cat belongs to," Jess added. "But we knew that this was the best place to bring the kittens!"

"I'm glad you did," said Lily, picking up one of the soft, wriggling creatures. It batted a paw at her dark hair, making them all laugh.

"The kittens will be fine with warmth and milk," Mr Hart said. He showed the

girls how to feed them with drops squeezed from tiny pipettes, then he and Mr Forester went into the house to join Mrs Hart for a cup of tea.

The kittens climbed over each other, trying to reach the milk.

"They're greedy!" laughed Jess.

When they were full, the kittens cuddled together and fell asleep.

"I wonder who your mother is," said Lily, stroking a kitten with a white tip on its tail. "We already know one mysterious cat, don't we, Jess?"

The two friends shared a smile, thinking of their magical cat friend, Goldie. She

came from Friendship Forest, a secret world of talking animals, and had taken the girls on adventures there. An evil witch called Grizelda wanted to drive the animals out of the forest so she could have it for herself, and Lily and Jess had helped stop her on several occasions.

"I wonder when we'll see Goldie again," said Jess.

As soon as she had spoken, the girls heard a soft *tap-tap-tap* at the window. They looked up to see a beautiful cat pawing at the glass. She had golden fur and eyes as green as grass in morning sunshine.

"Goldie!" cried Lily, opening the window. "We were just thinking about you!"

The cat jumped down and rubbed against her leg, then against Jess's.

"You know what this means, don't you?" said Lily.

Jess nodded excitedly. "Whenever Goldie visits, it's time for another adventure in Friendship Forest!"

Goldie mewed at them. The girls knew she wanted them to follow her!

"We're coming, Goldie," cried Lily. She quickly checked that the kittens were all right and then the girls ran outside.

They followed Goldie over the stepping stones that crossed Brightley Stream, and into Brightley Meadow. Goldie ran over to the Friendship Tree and it immediately burst into life. New leaves sprang from the dried twigs and blossoms burst into bloom. Birds sang sweetly among the branches. The girls had seen this happen before, but they still grinned at each other, wide-eyed with delight.

Goldie patted some letters carved into the tree trunk. Jess and Lily knew what the letters said, and that if they spoke the words aloud, magic would begin!

They held hands and said together, "Friendship Forest!"

A door as high as the girls' shoulders appeared in the trunk. Lily reached for the leaf-shaped handle and opened it.

Shimmering golden light shone from inside. Ducking down, Jess and Lily followed Goldie through the door. They felt a familiar tingling sensation all over.

We're shrinking, Jess thought excitedly.

The light faded. They were in a sun-dappled clearing surrounded by tall trees. Around the edge were the little cottages where the animals of Friendship Forest lived.

"We're back!" said Lily, her brown eyes shining.

"And we're so glad you are," said a soft voice.

The girls turned to see Goldie standing upright, wearing a glistening scarf. Because the girls had shrunk, she now stood as tall as their shoulders.

Beside Goldie was a family of three tabby cats – two adults and a little kitten.

Their silvery fur was swirled with dark grey. The girls recognised the kitten – they had met her on their very first visit to Friendship Forest. She wore a rucksack on her back, and a pair of odd-looking binoculars dangled around her neck. She stared at the girls in amazement.

Goldie hugged Jess and Lily, then introduced them to the cats.

"This is Mr and Mrs Tabbypaw," she said. "As you girls know, I was once a stray in the human world. When I first found my way to Friendship Forest, the Tabbypaws looked after me. You're all very special to me, so I wanted you to meet each other."

"We're so pleased to meet you, Jess and Lily," said Mrs Tabbypaw. "You're such wonderful friends to all the animals."

"Yes, indeedy," said Mr Tabbypaw. "We heard you stopped that witch from ruining our lovely forest. Three times, in fact!"

"Dad! Dad!" said the kitten.

"Ah, this is Bella," said Mr Tabbypaw. "She's excited to meet you properly too!"

"I saw you when you first came to Friendship Forest!" said the kitten. "We live far away in Buttercup Grove, and guess what? Tonight I'm having my first ever sleepover in Goldie's Grotto!'

Mr and Mrs Tabbypaw had to leave so they'd be home before dark. They hugged and kissed Bella.

"Goodbye, Jess and Lily," they said. "It was wonderful to meet you. Bye, Goldie!'

They disappeared into the trees.

"Let's go to the Toadstool Café," Goldie said.

"Ooh, yes!" said Bella. "Jess and Lily, can you come, too? And to the sleepover?

TOADSTOOL
CAFÉ

Can you? You could tell me stories about your world. I love hearing about new things. Please?"

"You would be very welcome," smiled Goldie.

Jess looked at Lily. "What about it?" she said. "Time stands still while we're in Friendship Forest, remember? We can stay as long as we like."

"We'd love to!" said Lily.

Bella danced around in a circle and cheered. "Hooray!"

CHAPTER TWO

Strange Sounds

Bella chattered as they made their way to the Toadstool Café.

"I love exploring," she said, peering at the wild flowers growing around the clearing. "Ooh! A bumblebee! Have you ever seen so many stripes?"

"Take a closer look with your

binoculars," Lily suggested.

Bella giggled. "These aren't binoculars," she said. "They're night-goggles for seeing in the dark. Mr Cleverfeather, the owl, invented them."

"When Bella grows up she'll have perfect night-vision, like me," Goldie explained, "but she can't see properly in the dark yet."

Lily was about to reply when she heard a grunt. "What was that?" she asked. "It came from behind that starflower bush."

Jess went to look, but didn't see anyone. "That's strange," she said.

Soon they arrived at the Toadstool Café. The tables and umbrellas dotted around outside were too small for the girls, so they sat on the mossy ground instead. As Bella ran around exploring the glade, Goldie came over to talk to the girls.

"Jess, Lily," she said quietly. "Remember that grunt we heard, from behind the starflower bush?"

They nodded.

"Earlier today," Goldie continued, "the Tabbypaws and I heard strange sounds in the forest, rather like that grunt."

Jess frowned. "Could it have been the Boggits?"

The Boggits were the mean, filthy servants of Grizelda the witch. She'd promised the Boggits a dirty, muddy new home if they helped her get rid of all the animals in Friendship Forest.

Before Goldie could reply, there was a loud crash from inside the café. She ran inside, while Jess and Lily kneeled to peer through the doorway.

Mr and Mrs Longwhiskers, the owners of the café, were scratching their ears and staring at a heap of saucepans on the floor.

"Whatever happened?" Mrs Longwhiskers wondered aloud. "They were on the draining board by the window a second ago."

The cat's ears twitched thoughtfully as she came back outside to join the girls. "Something strange is going on in Friendship Forest," Goldie said. "I wonder what?"

An hour later, Goldie, Bella and the girls arrived at Goldie's grotto. It was a cave in another beautiful clearing. Beside the cave grew the Blossom Briar, a tall bush with colourful flowers as big as footballs. The girls knew that the Blossom Briar was connected to every flower in Friendship Forest. As long as it was healthy, the flowers would bloom too.

Goldie opened the red front door that had a window the shape of a letter G, and they all went inside. On the mossy floor was a comfy bed, a squishy armchair, a table and a fat round footstool.

They ate pumpkin and pine nut soup with wild garlic bread, then curled up on the floor in a nest of quilts, blankets and heaps of soft cushions. Bella put her night-goggles into her rucksack and hung it on a hook, then clambered onto Jess's lap.

"It's so cosy and comfortable," said Jess, stroking the kitten.

Bella started to purr. "Tell me stories about the human world!" she said.

Lily told Bella all about the wildlife hospital. When she'd finished, Bella said, "More!" so Jess told tales about school and the funny things their teacher said.

"More! More!" said Bella.

"I know," said Goldie, "I'll tell you the legend of Friendship Forest."

"What's a legend?" asked Bella.

"A very old story," said Goldie, "but we don't know if it's really true."

"Ooh!" said Bella.

So Goldie began. "Deep beneath Friendship Forest are many long-lost tunnels . . . "

"Wow!" said Bella, eyes wide. "Who lives there?"

"Nobody knows," said Goldie. "The legend tells that the tunnels are filled with wonderful jewels, some as small as apple pips, and some as big as a kitten!"

"I'd love to explore the tunnels and find some jewels," said Bella dreamily. She yawned and wriggled into a tighter ball. In moments, she was asleep.

Goldie giggled. "I'll finish that legend another time."

Jess carefully lifted Bella out of her lap and onto a quilt. Her paws twitched. "I think she's dreaming," Jess whispered with a grin.

The girls and Goldie snuggled down too. They were just drifting off when they heard a rough, gruff sound outside.

"Hegga hegga!" it went.

Jess and Lily sat bolt upright. What was that?

Goldie's ears pricked. "Girls," she whispered. "I think something's outside!"

Jess leaped up and ran outside, followed by Lily and Goldie. She spotted a shadowy shape among the trees.

"Over there!" Jess pointed, but the

shadow had gone.

They went back inside, and Goldie made mugs of hot honey-milk.

Bella snuffled softly. She hadn't heard a thing.

"That was strange," Lily murmured as they settled back among the blankets. She stroked the sleeping kitten anxiously. "I hope Grizelda and her Boggits aren't back in the forest." Her mind whirring, Lily drifted off into an uneasy sleep.

CHAPTER THREE

Footprints

The next morning, Lily woke first. When she saw the cave roof, she wondered where she was. Then she remembered.

Goldie's grotto, she thought with a smile. *I wonder if Bella's awake yet.*

She rolled over to see. But Bella wasn't there.

Lily shook Jess and Goldie awake. "I can't find Bella," she told them.

"She's probably burrowed under the covers," said Goldie.

They searched among the quilts and blankets and called Bella's name. But there was no sign of the little kitten.

Jess's hands flew to her mouth. "She's gone!" she cried.

Lily pointed to an empty hook. "Her rucksack's disappeared too," she exclaimed.

Lily went pale. "Remember the noises we heard last night? Maybe Bella woke up and heard them too, and went to find out what was making them!"

Goldie's whiskers twitched with worry. "Let's hurry back to Toadstool Glade," she said. "If Bella's gone off exploring, someone might have seen her."

She grabbed her scarf. Outside, they saw that it had rained heavily in the night. Raindrops sparkled on the leaves of the Blossom Briar.

"I hope poor Bella didn't get soaked," said Lily as they hurried after Goldie.

At Toadstool Glade, Goldie jumped on

a log and called to all the animals. "Has anyone seen Bella Tabbypaw?"

"Not since yesterday," said Mrs Twinkletail the mouse.

Mrs Longwhiskers nodded. "The last time we saw her was when she left for the sleepover."

Goldie frowned thoughtfully. "Has anyone heard anything strange in the forest? Or seen anything odd? It might help us find out where Bella is."

A duckling wearing red wellies waddled forwards. It was Ellie Featherbill! The girls had stopped Grizelda and her Boggits

from spoiling Willowtree River, where the Featherbills lived. Ellie's seven brothers and sisters, also wearing brightly coloured wellies, waddled after her.

"We've just been playing in puddles," Ellie said shyly. "My brother Stanley saw footprints in the mud. Big ones! Come and see!"

When Goldie and the girls reached the spot in the forest where the ducklings were playing, they found four sets of large footprints, and one set of tiny pawprints.

They stared at each other in horror.

"There's only one kind of creature that could have made those big prints," said Goldie grimly. "Boggits!"

"Four Boggits and Bella," said Lily in dismay. "Do you think they've kidnapped her, like they did to Lucy Longwhiskers?"

"I'm afraid it looks like it," said Goldie.

"Come on," said Jess.

"We've got to get Bella back!"

They thanked the Featherbill ducklings for their help and set off to follow the prints through the forest. They were soon deep among the trees.

"Let's hurry," said Goldie, glancing up at the sky. "It looks like it's going to rain again."

Sure enough, moments later, fat raindrops began to fall.

"We'll be wet through soon," said Lily, shaking water from her fringe.

Jess stopped and pointed. "Oh, no – the rain's washing the footprints away!"

To their dismay, the prints were disappearing before their eyes. They hurried on, now unsure if they were going the right way.

"Where can Bella be?" Lily wondered

aloud. "She must be so scared." She stopped to peer through the falling rain. "There aren't so many trees here, are there? It's almost as if we're coming to—"

"The edge of Friendship Forest!" said Goldie in alarm. "I've never been this far before. Oh, girls, I'm so sorry. I don't know where Bella is, and I don't know where we are either! This place smells horrible."

Jess comforted the tearful cat while Lily took a look around. She pushed through straggly bushes and gasped as her foot sank into something squishy.

Before her was a vast, oozing pool of runny, yellow-brown mud. Bubbles rose to the surface and popped, sending up stinking greenish clouds of gas. It smelled like old drains.

"Help!" she cried. "My foot's stuck in a swamp!"

CHAPTER FOUR

Boulder Barrier

"Lily! Hold on!" Jess cried.

Goldie grasped Jess around the waist to stop her slipping into the swamp too, and Jess reached out a hand to Lily. Lily clutched it. Together, Jess and Goldie pulled her free of the swamp.

Lily pushed back her dripping hair

and wiped mud off her trousers with wet leaves. "Thank you!" she said. "But now we're filthy, as well as soaked!"

Jess used a stick to scrape her trainer clean and Goldie shook glistening water droplets from her fur.

"Now what?" Lily said. "We can't go any further, because of the swamp."

"The Boggits and Bella can't have come this way either. Let's go back to where we last saw footprints," Jess suggested.

It had stopped raining, but they had to splash through lots of puddles on their way back to where the prints had been.

"I definitely saw a print here," said Jess, stopping.

The path split into three directions. One led to the swamp and another went back to the Toadstool Glade.

Goldie pointed down the third path. "They must have gone down there. Come on!"

The three friends ran along the path. It took them past thick, stumpy trees, across a leafy glade, and alongside a bubbling stream. They skittered down a slope between prickly berry bushes, but

found their way blocked by a huge heap of great grey boulders.

"It's a dead-end," groaned Lily. "They're not here."

"All this way for nothing," Jess said crossly. She went to sit on

the nearest boulder.

"Stop!" Lily cried, pulling her back.

"What's wrong?" asked Goldie.

"Look carefully at that boulder," said Lily.

Goldie and Jess peered at it.

"It's shimmering," said Goldie. "The boulder's magic!"

Lily reached out to feel it, but her hand passed right through! "It's all right," she said. "It doesn't hurt."

Goldie looked closer and gasped. "Girls, remember the legend I was telling you last night?" she said excitedly. "I think we've found the entrance to the Friendship Forest tunnels!"

Lily stared. "So it's true!"

"Why would the Boggits go in there?" Jess asked.

Lily frowned thoughtfully. "Remember the strange noises we heard right before the Longwhiskers' pans were knocked over? And then outside Goldie's grotto? Well, what if it was the Boggits snooping around, looking for mischief?" she said. "They would have heard Goldie talking about the jewels in the tunnels."

Jess nodded. "I think you're right – they might have decided to find the jewels! But why would they have taken Bella?"

"I don't know," said Goldie, "but we've got to go into the tunnel if we're going to get her back!"

They passed through the boulder with a shivery feeling and into the dark tunnel.

"I'll go first," said Goldie. "My cat's eyes give me excellent night vision, remember?"

She held one end of her scarf, told Lily to hold the middle and gave the other end to Jess. "Now we won't get separated in the dark," she explained.

They crept along the tunnel. Jess and Lily felt unsteady on the rough, uneven ground. It was strange not being able to

see their feet properly.

A loud noise rang out from up ahead, echoing through the tunnels.

The three friends clung together.

"Boggits?" Lily whispered.

The sound came again, closer this time.

Goldie's ears twitched. "It's someone laughing!" she said.

There was the pounding of running feet, coming nearer.

Goldie and the girls pressed themselves against the cold tunnel wall.

Lily clutched Jess's hand. "Whatever is it?" she whispered.

"I don't know," Jess replied in a shaky voice.

The laughter grew louder, and shadowy shapes seemed to be moving towards them.

"Hello!" said two high little voices.

Lily and Jess sighed in relief as they peered through the gloom.

The loud, echoing noise had been made by a pair of cheeky-looking fox cubs!

CHAPTER FIVE:

Glow in the Dark

"Girls," exclaimed Goldie, "meet Ruby and Rusty Fuzzybrush! But what are you two doing here?"

"We use the tunnels as our secret hiding place," said Ruby. "Mum and Dad don't know about them, so please don't tell." She put down two unlit lanterns she'd been holding.

"How did you get in?" asked Jess. *Maybe the fox cubs found the magical entrance, too,* she thought to herself.

"We know lots of ways," said Rusty, "but they're all hidden. That's why nobody else comes here."

"Somebody else has found a way in, I'm afraid," said Goldie. She explained about Bella and the Boggits. "If you know the tunnels well," she added, "will you help us find Bella?"

The fox cubs agreed immediately. "What an adventure!" said Rusty excitedly, picking up the lanterns. "These might be useful. Mr Cleverfeather invented them."

Jess and Lily took one each and looked for a way to turn them on.

"Where's the switch?" Jess asked.

The fox cubs laughed so much they fell over. "There's no switch for glow-worms!" giggled Ruby. "Watch!"

She put her mouth close to Jess's lantern and whispered, "Wakey, wakey, little glow-worms. Rise and shine! It's glowtime!"

Instantly, there was a soft glimmer that grew brighter and brighter until the

tunnel was filled with yellow light.

"Wow!" said Lily. She whispered to the glow-worms in her lantern. "Wakey, wakey, rise and shine! It's glowtime!" She laughed in delight as her lantern lit up too. The tunnel wasn't so scary now that she could see clearly.

They were about to set off again when a great gruff shout echoed down the tunnel.

"Boggits!" said Goldie, clutching at Jess and Lily. A moment later, there was a crashing sound and the whole tunnel seemed to shudder.

"It's an earthquake!" Lily whispered fearfully.

There was another crash. She covered her ears to shut out the noise.

The lanterns went dark.

"Oh, no!" Jess said. "The noise must have frightened the glow-worms. It's too dark to go any further without them."

"Glow-worms," Lily whispered, "don't be frightened. It's just a noise and we won't let it hurt you. Please wakey wakey."

There was the smallest gleam of light.

"Please?" begged Lily. "Rise and shine?"

Rusty crept across. "Hey, wormies!" he whispered. "We're desperate."

There was a tiny glimmer, then another, then another. Soon the lantern was filled with glowing lights, and the girls could see again.

"What are the Boggits up to?" said Goldie. "I'm so worried about Bella! Rusty and Ruby, I know it's scary but please take us through the tunnels so we can look for her."

Rusty and Ruby darted away.

As the others followed, Jess noticed that the light from the glow-worms was

casting huge shadows

on the tunnel walls. *What are they?* she wondered with a flutter of fear. Then she realised! "The fox cubs' shadows make them seem like giants!" she laughed.

Ruby and Rusty heard. They waved their paws and lashed their tails, making their shadows look like angry monsters!

The tunnel twisted and turned, then widened out. The friends found themselves at the opening of a vast cavern, with a thin, pale shaft of light filtering through a small hole in the roof. In the middle were four grubby, hairy creatures, covered in fur of sickly yellow, washed-out blue and dingy green.

Boggits!

"But where's Bella?" whispered Goldie.

Lily and Jess peered around the cavern. When the Boggits had kidnapped Lucy Longwhiskers, they had locked her inside a cage. What had they done with Bella?

Then, to their surprise, Bella walked out from behind one of the Boggits, wearing her night-goggles and rucksack, whistling happily!

CHAPTER SIX

A Terrible Plan

"At least Bella's okay," whispered Jess. "But why is she with the Boggits? And what are they doing down here?'

Lily asked the glow-worms to switch off and the glow faded. They all hid beneath an overhanging rock so they could spy on the Boggits without being seen. They could make out lots of tall, thick, stone pillars through the gloom that looked as if they were holding up the cavern roof.

"Those pillars are blocking the view," whispered Lily. She jumped as a Boggit laughed.

"Haargh! Haargh!'

Rusty sniffed. "Pooh, those Boggits stink!"

"Like rotting cauliflowers," Jess agreed in disgust. "Are they searching for jewels? Can you see what they're up to, Goldie?"

"Yes," said the cat. "Whiffy's scratching herself, Reek is picking his nose, and Sniff and Pongo are carrying huge stones."

Pongo's voice echoed around the cavern. "Oi, pussycat," he grunted to Bella, "put goggles on and tell Boggits where cracks are in pillars."

Bella stopped whistling. "All right," she said. After a moment, she continued, "This one's cracked."

Pongo bashed the pillar hard with his stone.

"Hegga, hegga!" chuckled Sniff. "Pussycat can see cracks with goggles. Clever Sniff to think of bringing pussycat to tunnels."

"Are we going to get some jewels

now?" Bella was pointing upwards. "You promised you'd help me find some jewels if I helped you with my night-goggles."

Jess glanced at the cave ceiling, where Bella was pointing. She gasped. "Look, Lily! Goldie, see there? On the cavern roof?"

"It's glittering!" whispered Lily.

"Jewels!" breathed Goldie. "The roof is studded with them, just like the legend said!"

"Poor Bella," whispered Lily. "She must have left Goldie's grotto to go exploring and bumped into the Boggits. They've tricked her into helping them!"

"But why are the Boggits smashing the pillars?" Jess wondered.

Whiffy gave another pillar a bash. "Boggits are right under Toadstool Glade. When pillars fall, Toadstool Glade will crash down. Bang! Smash! All animals' nasty cottages fall to bits! Grizelda be pleased!"

Jess, Lily and Goldie clutched one another in horror!

"This is Grizelda's most terrible plan yet!" gasped Lily. "All the animals' homes will be destroyed. They'll have to leave the forest and Grizelda will have it for herself!"

Goldie quickly explained what was happening to Ruby and Rusty. "To save Friendship Forest, we've got to stop the Boggits from smashing those pillars," she said urgently.

Jess glanced at her lantern. "Lily," she said, "remember how the glow-worms' light cast big shadows on the wall?"

Lily nodded.

"It's given me an idea for scaring away the Boggits," said Jess. "A shadow monster!"

"Brilliant!" said Lily. "But we mustn't scare Bella." She thought for a moment. "I know! Quiet, everyone!"

She picked up a stone and threw it as far as possible across the cavern. As she heard it land, the Boggits turned towards it. They'd heard it, too.

"What be that?" asked Whiffy.

"Boggits look," said Pongo. "Come on."

All four lumbered towards where the stone had landed.

In a flash, Lily darted out and scooped Bella up. The little kitten gave a happy

squeak and started purring.

"Hi, Lily—" Bella started to say, but Lily hushed her.

She darted back behind the rock, where Jess and Goldie hugged Bella with relief.

"Thank goodness you're safe!" said

Goldie. She explained that the Boggits had tricked Bella into helping them with their plan.

Bella was horrified. "Knock the cottages down? Destroy Toadstool Glade?" she whispered. "I thought they were being nice. They mustn't ruin the village!"

"You're right," said Jess. "And we need a brave little explorer to help stop them."

CHAPTER SEVEN

Monster!

Jess whispered in Bella's ear.

The kitten's eyes grew wide.

"Go on," said Jess, when she'd finished. "Goggles on, you brave explorer."

Bella scampered to the middle of the cavern just as the Boggits returned, grumbling about mystery noises.

"Boggits!" cried Bella. "I've remembered something scary."

Reek snorted. "Boggits isn't scared."

The others laughed. "Haargh! Haargh!"

"Ssh!" said Bella. "You'll wake it."

"Wake what?" growled Reek.

"The monster!" said Bella. "The Boggit-eating monster!"

"No such thing," Pongo scoffed.

But Sniff grunted nervously. "What if there really is monster?"

Whiffy looked down. "Whiffy's knees is knocking."

"No monster," Pongo growled.

"Pussycat, find cracked pillars. Boggits, get bashing!"

Beneath the overhanging rock, Jess explained her plan to the others.

"Bella's given them the idea of a monster," she whispered. "Now it's up to us to make one!"

They gathered in a line, arms round one another's middles. Lily and Jess were at the top, so the shadow monster would have two heads and four front legs. The fox cubs were next, so it seemed to have eight more little legs. Goldie was at the back, bent over like a great hump.

When Bella saw Lily give the thumbs-up, she sneaked back over.

Lily whispered, "Wakey, wakey, little glow-worms. Rise and shine! It's glowtime!" and handed the lanterns to the plucky kitten.

Bella crept back to the Boggits.

The lantern's light grew from a

glimmer to a golden glow. Bella shone it on the friends, casting a huge monster-shadow on the wall.

Lily and Jess roared and wobbled their heads, making the shadow heads rear back and forth. The fox cubs stamped and howled.

"Aaaargh!" screeched Reek.

"Monster attack!" shrieked Pongo. "Run!"

The shadow monster roared and lashed its tail.

"Don't eat me!" begged Sniff. "Eat Whiffy!"

"No! I

be thin and bony,"

bellowed Whiffy. "Eat Sniff!

Sniff be tasty!"

They fought, pushed and scrambled to escape the monster. At last, they found a tunnel and stampeded down it, shrieking.

The group of friends, with Bella in tow, followed the Boggits down one tunnel, then another, roaring and howling.

Goldie sniffed. "There's a horrible smell coming from up ahead," she called over the roars.

"That's the swamp," cried Rusty. "It's all mud and stink."

"If we can chase them into it," Lily said, "maybe they'll be so happy to find mud that they won't come back to smash the pillars!"

"Great idea," said Jess.

Roaring and howling some more, the shadow monster lurched on down the tunnel behind the Boggits. They thundered along, shrieking in fright, and ran out into the grey light.

Lily, Jess, Goldie and the others waited in the tunnel until the Boggits' yells died down. Then they crept outside. The

Boggits were tramping into the swamp.

Pongo spotted them and roared in fury. "Boggits been tricked!" he bellowed. "Get them!"

But the other Boggits ignored him.

Whiffy grabbed handfuls of the gloop oozing around her. "Lovely!" she said, rubbing it into her fur.

Sniff and Reek sloshed mud over each other.

"Better than Boggits' muddy pool," said Reek happily. He flung himself on his back and sank into the mud, shouting, "LOVELY swamp!" He stood up, gloop oozing down his nose.

Even Pongo agreed. "Swamp is enormous," he said and dived in head first. "Wheeee!"

"I think we're safe," Jess whispered. "Goldie, the Boggits love the swamp so much, perhaps we can talk them into staying here?"

Lily hugged her. "That's brilliant!" she said. "Grizelda was going to give them a new home if they ruined Friendship Forest, so they'd obviously be happy to move."

"It's a wonderful idea," Goldie agreed. "If they're happy here, they'd have no reason to do what Grizelda wants. But it will take some work to turn the swamp into the perfect Boggit home. We're going to need help."

"Send a flyer," suggested Jess. "Lots of flyers!"

Goldie put her paws together like

wings, and

fluttered them. The

fox cubs and Bella did the same,

then Jess and Lily fluttered their hands.

A moment later, a large yellow butterfly perched on Goldie's shoulder.

"Hello, Flitta," said the cat.

A purple butterfly settled on Goldie's other shoulder.

"Hi, Hermia," said Jess, remembering her from their adventure rescuing Molly Twinkletail.

Soon they were surrounded by a cloud of butterflies. Their rainbow colours swirled as they danced around each other, chattering in tiny, tinkly voices. Jess and Lily caught some of what they were saying.

"That smell! Oh, dear!"

"I know! Enough to make your wings droop."

"You can see why," trilled another. "B-O-G-G-I-T-S."

Goldie giggled. "Butterflies," she said, "please ask all the animals to bring supplies – anything suitable for a Boggit home."

As the butterflies flew away, the girls heard Hermia tell Flitta, "The animals won't have to think very hard. They can just bring their rubbish bins!" and they both laughed.

CHAPTER EIGHT

Home, Stinky Home

Later, Jess and Lily helped Mr Cleverfeather put the roof on a hut for the Boggits. He'd brought a new invention, the Lifter-upper. As Jess sat on a seat and pedalled madly, the Lifter-upper raised the roof. Lily pushed a lever, and the roof moved directly above the hut.

Mr Cleverfeather pressed a button. Down it dropped. *Bang!*

The Featherbills laid a carpet of slimy pondweed from near their river barge.

"Urgh, it's yucky," said Ellie Featherbill.

"Boggits love yuck," Lily giggled. "And muck."

Other animals heaped rubbish around the hut. Pongo looked at it fondly, as Reek and Sniff splashed in the mud, Bella and the fox cubs rolling about beside them.

"The smell doesn't bother you after a while," yelled Rusty, laughing.

Just then Mr Cleverfeather called, "The

rut's heady – er, I mean the hut's ready!"

"Not ready," Whiffy grunted. "Hut needs mud." She scooped up fistfuls of swamp goo and threw it over the roof.

The other Boggits joined in happily.

Reek grunted. "Girls and cat find swamp. Girls good!"

Sniff grinned. "Cat good!"

"Mud good!" cried Whiffy.

Pongo turned to Bella. "Pussycat want to help?"

Everybody wanted to help!

Suddenly, Lily's eye was caught by an orb of light floating across the swamp.

"Grizelda!" she cried. "Grizelda's here!"

The animals shrieked and ran to huddle behind Goldie and the girls.

The orb hovered, then, with a flash and a *cra-ack*, it burst in a shower of yellow sparks. In its place stood the witch, wearing her shiny purple tunic and trousers, and her boots with their sharply pointed toes. Her green hair swirled around her head like snakes.

"Boggits!" she screeched. "Get back to work. Go and smash those pillars!"

There was a moment's silence. The Boggits muttered together.

"Oh, no," Lily whispered. "They're going to obey her."

"We can't let them," said Jess. "Boggits!" she yelled. "You have a new home. You don't need to do what she says!"

Pongo looked at Jess. He looked at the dirty new hut. Then he turned to Grizelda. "No!" he shouted. "Boggits not helping ANY more!"

Reek lumbered forward. "Grizelda smash pillars herself," he growled.

"What!" shrieked Grizelda. "Me? Work? Are you mad? You do it!"

Lily and Jess held their breath. Would

the Boggits give in?

"No!" Whiffy snapped, peering from behind Sniff.

Grizelda screamed, "If you want a new home, get rid of the animals first—"

"No!" said Pongo. "Boggits is happy in swamp. Go away!"

Grizelda's hair whipped the air. Her face was dark with rage. "I won't give up," she snarled. "Friendship Forest will be mine!"

She snapped her fingers and vanished in a shower of hissing red sparks.

The animals cheered. "Hooray for the Boggits!"

"Thank goodness she's gone," said Lily, then she gasped. "But what about the damage the Boggits did to the cavern? What if they've already done enough to harm the forest?"

"Oh, we stopped them before any serious damage was done," said Goldie. "I'll go and check later to make sure, but

I think Toadstool Glade will be just fine."

"Hurrah! The forest is safe!" Lily cried.

But Jess noticed a flicker of worry cross Goldie's face. "What is it?" she asked.

"I think Grizelda meant what she said," Goldie said nervously. "She won't give up until she has the forest for herself."

Lily gave her a hug. "Then we'll do our best to stop her. We promise!"

Jess hugged Goldie too. "You can count on us!"

The animals waved goodbye to the Boggits, then set off home. The Boggits sat in the swamp, patting mud into their fur. They grinned at Goldie and the girls, showing their filthy teeth.

"I can't believe we're sort-of friends with them now," Lily giggled.

"Me neither," said Jess. "They're all right when they're not obeying Grizelda, aren't they? Dirty, of course."

"And smelly," Lily said.

"And hideous and lumpy," said Goldie.

"But kind of nice, too," Jess added, and they laughed.

It was time to leave the swamp. Jess picked up a purring Bella and Lily held the fox cubs' paws. Overhead, the butterflies fluttered like a rainbow cloud.

Back in Toadstool Glade, the animals threw a party to celebrate. There was lots of yummy food from the Toadstool Café and everyone danced to music coming from a strange box that Mr Cleverfeather called his Melody-o-Matic. Lily, Jess and Goldie whirled around. Bella swished her tail in time to the music and the Longwhiskers family danced the bunny bump, which included lots of hopping.

Eventually, it was time for Lily and Jess to go home.

"My mum and dad won't believe how much exploring I did," said Bella as they gave her a farewell cuddle. "Thank you for rescuing me."

"You're very welcome," said Lily. They waved goodbye to their other friends and followed Goldie to the Friendship Tree at the centre of the forest.

When they reached it, Goldie said, "I'm so proud of you for helping to stop Grizelda. When I first saw you at the wildlife hospital, I knew I could count on such brave, kind girls." She hugged them.

"We've had such wonderful adventures," said Jess.

"I'll come back for you soon," Goldie promised. She touched a paw to the tree and a door appeared in the trunk. "Goodbye for now, girls!"

"Goodbye!" said Lily and Jess. Holding hands, they stepped through the door and into the golden light. When it faded, they were back in Brightley Meadow.

"What an amazing adventure," sighed Jess as they went over the stepping stones and back to Helping Paw. "I'm so glad the forest is safe."

"Me too," agreed Lily.

Although the girls had been gone all night and much of that day, no time had passed in their world. At the wildlife hospital, the kittens were just waking up.

"They're so cute," said Lily. "The smallest one looks a bit like Bella, doesn't she?"

"She does," said Jess. "Oh, Lily, she's so sweet. I wish—"

She stopped as the door opened, and Mr Forester came in, clutching his mug of tea.

"Jess, I've been thinking," he said. "We'll need to find homes for all these kittens.

Maybe one of them could live with us."

She threw her arms around him. "Oh, thanks, Dad!" she cried. "I'd really love the tiny one!'

Lily lifted the kitten into Jess's hands. As the little creature purred, the girls shared a secret smile. What a magical day!

The End

Have the girls defeated Grizelda once and for all?

Catch a glimpse of the next Magic Animal Friends adventure,

Poppy Muddlepup's Daring Rescue

Turn over for a sneak peek . . .

"We're trapped!" cried Lily. "But why?"

"Gretchen, what have you done?" said Jess, horrified.

The pretty face appeared above the spiky cage. Gretchen seemed to have grown taller. Then, to the girls' horror, yellow-green sparks crackled around her. The marmalade-coloured hair turned green, and the pretty dress became a swirling black cloak.

"It's Grizelda!" cried Lily. "Gretchen was the witch in disguise. She's tricked us!"

Grizelda's awful cackle echoed round

the forest. "Haa haaa haaaa! You fools! You're always visiting Toadstool Glade, so I knew that if I waited there you'd show up before long. And now you've told me exactly what you're up to!"

Jess and Lily stared at her in horror.

The witch laughed again. "You won't find the water, and you'll never find the Sunrise Berries . . ."

Read

Poppy Muddlepup's Daring Rescue

to find out what happens next!

Magic Animal Friends

Read all the Magic Animal Friends adventures and be part of the secret!

Series One

COMING SOON!

Look out for
Jess and Lily's
next adventure –
with adorable puppy
Poppy Muddlepup!

3 stories in 1!

www.magicanimalfriends.com

Puzzle Fun!

One of our Magic Animal Friends
is hiding in this picture.

Can you join the dots to discover who it is?

Lily and Jess's Animal Care Tips

Lily and Jess love helping lots of different animals – both in Friendship Forest and in the real world.

Here are their top tips for looking after...

CATS

like Bella Tabbypaw

- Cats are very playful animals. If you have a pet cat, make sure you play with them lots! Playtime is also a good way for your cat to get exercise too!

- All cats like milk but it is not good for them to have too much of it.

- Cats like to roam over a wide area. If you find a cat that you think might be a stray the best thing to do is to ask around the neighbourhood to see if anyone knows who the cat you have seen belongs to.